THE LITTLE TRAIN

THE LITTLE TRAIN

LOIS LENSKI

Random House New York

Engineer Small has a little train. The engine is black and shiny. He keeps it oiled and polished.

Engineer Small is proud of his little engine. The engine has a bell and a whistle. It has a sand dome. It has a headlight and a smokestack. It has four big driving wheels. It has a firebox under its boiler. When the water in the boiler is heated, it makes steam. Steam makes the engine go.

The little engine lives in the roundhouse. Engineer Small backs it out onto the turntable. The turntable moves around with it. Then the engine moves off onto the track. It pulls a tender behind it.

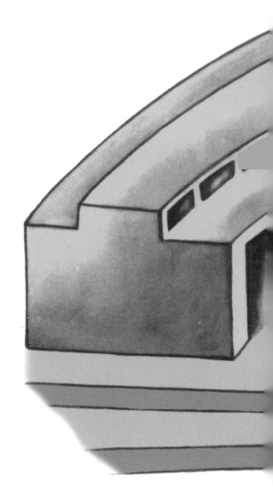

The little train is going on a journey to the city. Fireman Shorty helps to get it ready. The engine comes to a water column beside the track. The water column has a large spout.

Fireman Shorty climbs out on top of the tender. He puts the spout over the water tank. He turns the water on. *Splash!* The water flows into the tank. When it is full, Shorty turns the water off.

Now the little engine is beside the coal hopper. A long chute reaches down to the front part of the tender. Soon the coal rushes down the chute. *R-r-r-r-r! R-r-r-r-r!* It fills the tender full.

The rest of the train stands
waiting on the track. There is a
mail and baggage car.

There are two passenger cars.
The little engine backs up to them.

Bang! Bumpety bump! The cars
are hitched on behind.

The little engine pulls the train into the station. It huffs and puffs. It is ready to go. Mailbags are put into the mail car.

Baggage is put into the baggage car—
suitcases, boxes, and trunks. People buy
tickets in the station. They climb into the
passenger cars.

Huff! Huff! Huff! goes the engine. Engineer Small and Conductor Little look at their watches.

"Two minutes and we go!" says Engineer Small.

"Right you are!" answers Conductor Little.

They read their orders. The orders tell where the train is to go. Then Engineer Small climbs up into the cab.

"All aboard!" calls Conductor Little. He raises his hand and signals to the engineer. Then he too climbs aboard.

Engineer Small looks out the cab window. He sees Conductor Little's signal.

"Ready!" he says to Fireman Shorty. "Here we go!"

Fireman Shorty throws on a shovel of coal. Engineer Small pulls the whistle cord. *Toot! Toot!* He slowly opens the throttle. The wheels begin to move. *C-H-O-O! C-H-O-O! CHOO! CHOO!*

Engineer Small opens the throttle wider. Fireman Shorty shovels more coal on the fire. Black smoke pours from the smokestack. *Huff! Huff! Huff! Choo, choo, CHOO, CHOO!* Away goes the little train. *Who-o-o-o-o! Who-o-o-o-o!*

The little train comes to a crossing.
The bell begins to ring. *Ding, ding,
ding, ding, ding, ding!*

The gates drop down across the road. Automobiles stop.

The little train goes whizzing by. The gates swing up again. The automobiles can now cross over the track.

The little train goes faster and faster. Soon the station is left far behind. Engineer Small watches the track ahead for signals.

Soon he comes to a semaphore. It is a wooden arm on a tall post. The semaphore is turned straight up.

"Clear track ahead!" says Engineer Small. That means he does not have to stop. *Who-o-o-o! Who-o-o-o!* The little train goes on and on.

The little train passes farms and farmhouses.
It passes cows and horses in the fields. It passes
hills and woods and streams.

A boy on a fence waves his hand. Engineer Small waves back. Then he pulls the whistle cord. *Toot! Toot! Who-o-o-o! Who-o-o-o!* The little train goes on and on.

Engineer Small watches the signals ahead. He sees a semaphore halfway down. That is a caution signal. It means to go slowly because there is a train ahead. Engineer Small closes the throttle. He puts on the brakes. *P-ss-ss-ss! P-ss-ss-ss!* The little train slows down.

Soon Engineer Small sees a
semaphore pointing across. That
means he must stop. He must wait
until the train ahead goes on.
Engineer Small puts the brakes
on all the way. *P-ss-ss-sst!*
P-ss-ss-sst! The little train stops.
The little train waits.

Suddenly the semaphore flies up.

"Clear track again!" says Engineer Small.

"Let's go!" says Fireman Shorty.

Engineer Small opens the throttle. The little train starts. It goes very fast. The little train goes on and on.

The little train comes to a switch. It moves onto the siding and waits. Engineer Small and Fireman Shorty look out the cab window. Suddenly they hear a loud swish and roar. A great streamlined train rushes by. It is the Blue Streak Express. Off it goes in the distance. The little train leaves the siding. It goes on its way again.

A river runs along by the track. The little train comes to a drawbridge. The bridge is up. A sailboat is passing underneath.

Engineer Small puts his brakes on.
The little train stops and waits.

The drawbridge goes down. The train crosses over.

Just ahead there is a big dark hole in the side of the hill.

"Here's the tunnel, Shorty!" says Engineer Small. He looks at his watch. "Right on time!"

Whish! The little train goes into the hole. It is very black inside the tunnel. Only a spot of light can be seen far away at the end.

The little train comes out into the light again.
Now it is on the other side of the big hill. Soon it
comes to the city. The little train runs slowly.

It stops in the station. The passengers get off.
The baggage is taken off. The mail is taken off.
The little train has come to the end of the trip.

The little engine will go to the roundhouse. It will stay there all night. It will be made ready for the next trip. Engineer Small, Fireman Shorty, and Conductor Little go out the gates. They will sleep in the city all night. They will take the little train back to Tinytown in the morning.

And that's all —
About
Engineer Small !